1 The First Emperor of China

Qin Shihuangdi was a brilliant military leader who united the country. He lived from 259 to 210 BC and began the Great Wall of China. This image comes from a much later period and shows how people imagined he might have looked.

2 General and archer from the terracotta army

The First Emperor buried a huge terracotta army around his tomb.
The heads of the figures were individually modelled so that every one is slightly different.

3 Cavalryman with his horse

This horseman comes from the First Emperor's terracotta army. The emperor used 700,000 people
in the construction of his tomb, which took 38 years to build.

4 Dragon with a flaming pearl
The flaming pearl stands for knowledge and wards off evil. The five-clawed dragon symbolized the Chinese emperor during the Ming and Qing dynasties (1368-1911). In China dragons are considered to be very lucky.

5 Fish

The mandarin fish symbolizes wealth and prosperity. This one is painted on a dish made in the Yuan dynasty, in about 1340.

6 Boys riding hobby horses

Riding hobby horses was a popular pastime with Chinese children. Hobby horses represent fertility, wealth and happiness. This picture comes from a painted silk scroll of 'One Hundred Children' from the Ming dynasty, about 1545.

7 Chinese mansion among the clouds

A willow tree grows beside this mansion among the clouds. From a jar of the Ming dynasty, about 1510.

8 Fish dragon
This rare flying fish dragon chases the flaming pearl among the clouds.
From a dish of the Ming dynasty, about 1510.

9 Playing Chinese chess

Chess-playing was one of the four major arts of an educated man in China.
From a large jar of the Ming dynasty, about 1500.

10 Frog on a lily pad

The frog stares up at a butterfly. He is surrounded by plants, and a spider's web is hidden among the rushes.
The sun is coming out from behind a cloud. From a bowl of the Ming dynasty, about 1600.

11 Official on horseback

The official is followed by his attendant carrying a parasol. They are approaching the mansion shown in picture 7.
From a jar of the Ming dynasty, about 1500.

12 Two deer

The deer stand among the rocks, under a pine tree. Beyond is a pool and a waterfall.
Idyllic scenes of nature like this are typical of the time. From a dish of the Ming dynasty, made in about 1600.

13 Assistant to the Judge of Hell

The female assistant holds a book containing records of good deeds.
This ceramic figure was made in the Ming dynasty (1522-1620).

14 Two lion-dogs

Two Buddhist lion-dogs scampering among peonies. Lion-dogs are often associated with modern-day Pekingese dogs. The drawing is adapted from two sources: an abacus (counting machine) box and a jar, both of the Ming dynasty.

15 Dragon

A dragon from a dish of the Ming dynasty, about 1500. Dragons were said to control the earth
and the heavens, because they controlled the rains that nourished the crops.

16 Boy riding a water buffalo
The boy is riding beneath a pine tree, which symbolizes long life and steadfastness.
The water buffalo represents the coming of spring. Ming dynasty, about 1600.

The illustrations were drawn by Ann Searight

Published by British Museum Press
A division of the British Museum Company Ltd
38 Russell Square, London WC1B 3QQ

Second Impression 2007
ISBN-13: 978-0-7141-3123-8

Design and typesetting by John Hawkins Book Design
Printed by Oriental Press